SOME WOR
THIS D

"Can we go again!

can we!

☆

"Who's she calling Fly Face?"

A miffed lion

☆

"I just DO NOT believe it!!"

A cross Mum

☆

"Sorry, but I was busting."

An embarrassed rhino

A nod and a wink to Colchester Zoo

DAISY AND THE TROUBLE WITH ZOOS
A RED FOX BOOK 978 1 862 30493 2

First published in Great Britain by Red Fox,
an imprint of Random House Children's Books
A Random House Group Company

This edition published 2008

5 7 9 10 8 6 4

Set in Vag Rounded

Red Fox Books are published by Random House Children's Books,
61–63 Uxbridge Road, London W5 5SA

www.daisyclub.co.uk

Addresses for companies within The Random House Group Limited
can be found at: www.randomhouse.co.uk/offices.htm

THE RANDOM HOUSE GROUP Limited Reg. No. 954009

A CIP catalogue record for this book is available from the British Library.

Printed and bound in Great Britain by
CPI Bookmarque, Croydon, CR0 4TD

DAISY

and the TROUBLE with
ZOOS

by Kes Gray

RED FOX

Chapter 1

The **trouble with zoos** is they shouldn't say things they don't mean. Especially on seven-year-olds' birthdays. If zoos say things they don't mean on a seven-year-old's birthday, then anything can happen. Which is why what happened today DID happen. Which ISN'T my FAULT.

My mum says all the other seven-year-olds in the zoo knew what the zoo meant. Which is a lie. Because Gabby didn't understand what the zoo meant either and she's been seven for ages.

Dylan didn't even know! And he's as old as NINE!!!!!!!!!

Gabby and Dylan are my best friends, which is why Mum invited them to come to the zoo with me today. Going to the zoo was my special birthday treat!

The **trouble with special birthday treats** is they only happen once a year, which means they can make you a bit excited.

My mum says I hadn't got a BIT excited, I'd got OVER–OVER-excited. She says there's a big difference between being a bit excited and being over–over-excited, and that if I ever get over–over-excited like today again, then all my birthdays will be cancelled in future. Which means I'll be seven for ever.

Gabby and Dylan say that if my mum cancels all my birthdays, I can share some of theirs. Like for instance when Gabby has her next birthday, she gets half of it and I get the other half. That means, instead of Gabby being eight, she'll only go up a half to seven and a half, but I'll go up a half to seven and a half too!

Dylan says that he wants to keep three quarters of his birthday. That means on his next birthday, instead of being ten, he doesn't mind being nine and three quarters instead, which is nearly ten anyway.

Dylan says giving someone a quarter of your birthday is still quite a lot, especially when someone else has already given you one of their halves too. Plus, Dylan says if I can find another person to give me one of their quarters, then I'll be back to normal.

Except, the **trouble with me going back to normal** is it won't be right, because then I'll be going up in ones, Dylan will be going up in three quarters and Gabby will be going up in halves.

Which is less than me. Which really wouldn't be fair because I was the one that got over–over-excited at the zoo, not them.

Dylan says to make it fair, Gabby and him would need to find someone else to give them a half AND a quarter of their birthday!

BUT THAT adds up to three quarters of a birthday!!!

Dylan says that the **trouble with someone giving away three quarters of their birthday** is they'll only be getting a quarter older every year. Which really isn't very much at all.

Dylan is ever so good at maths. He's going to be a computer when he grows up.

Gabby isn't. Gabby hates adding up. And taking away. Gabby says sums make her brain shrink. The **trouble with your brain shrinking** is in the end it will turn into a pea.

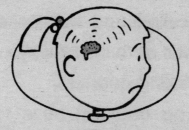

Which is the worst thing in the world a brain could turn into.

Plus your head will start to rattle.

And you won't be able to tie your shoe laces.

Or do joined up.

In the end we all agreed it would be easier if I didn't EVER get over–over-excited in zoos again. That way, what happened today will never happen again.

Plus none of my birthdays will ever get cancelled and we can all grow up in ones on our birthdays, instead of halves and quarters.

Plus no one will have to worry about blowing out more than their fair share of candles.

Or getting too many pink ones.

Gabby says just to make sure I don't get over–over-excited again, it might be better if I didn't ever go to the zoo again. EVER EVER!

Gabby said maybe we should just go swimming or something on my next birthday.

But I said no way.

Swimming pools aren't any-where near as good as zoos. Even swimming pools with slides and wave machines and hot chocolates.

And anyway. What happened today WASN'T MY FAULT!

IT WAS THE ZOO'S FAULT!

Chapter 2

Do you always wake up early on your birthday? I do. Especially when I've got presents to open AND a special birthday treat with an extra-special secret surprise to find out about too!

The **trouble with special birthday treats with an extra-special secret surprise** is they make you wake up even earlier than early.

I'm not sure exactly what time it was when I woke my mum up the first time this morning. But by the third time it was 2:27.

It felt much much later than that to me. In fact it felt just like the afternoon at 2:27 this morning to me!

And at 2:49, 3:17, 3:25 and 3:33!

By 3:34 Mum's voice had gone all growly. I couldn't see her because it was too dark in the bedroom, but I recognized her growly voice.

She always does growly voices when she's grumpy.

That's the **trouble with mums at 3:34 in the morning**: they just don't care about other people's birthdays.

Mum said she did care about my birthday, but 3:34 wasn't the morning, it was the middle of the night and I should go back to bed, get under my covers, close my eyes, fall asleep and come and wake her at eight o'clock.

"Or else."

I said or else what?

She said or else I wouldn't get any birthday presents in the morning at all. I said maybe the clock in her bedroom was wrong.

She said the clock in her bedroom was never wrong. It was digital. She said digital clocks are never wrong. Especially at 3:34 in the morning. I said it was afternoon in Australia.

She said we don't live in Australia.

I said I wished we did.

She said sometimes she wished I did too.

I said, "Can't I open just one of my presents?"

She said if I didn't go back to bed RIGHT NOW, I wouldn't get any presents OR my special birthday treat OR my extra-special secret birthday surprise EITHER!

So I went back to bed.

The **trouble with going back to bed when you don't want to** is your eyelids won't close.

Well, they will close, but they won't stay closed. That's because eyelids are one of the most excited bits of your body.

I closed mine about a trillion times, but every time I thought of my presents, or wondered what my secret birthday special surprise was, they just kept pinging open again.

I even tried holding them down with my fingers, but that didn't work either. That's the **trouble with holding eyelids down with your fingers.** If your eyelids are too excited, you have to let go.

The **trouble with letting go of your eyelids when they are too excited** is your eyeballs start getting excited next.

Then your head. And then your whole body. Including your pyjamas.

If Mum had let me open just one of my presents, then I would probably have been all right. I would probably have gone straight back to sleep. My eyeballs wouldn't have got excited, my eyelids wouldn't have kept pinging open, and my whole body wouldn't have been so wriggly.

But she didn't. And they did.

That's the **trouble with not being allowed to open just ONE present**: the only thing you CAN open IS your eyes.

I didn't go to sleep at all after that.

Chapter 3

When my mum woke me up, it was half-past eight!

"Happy birthday, Daisy!" she said. "Wake up, Sleepy Head! It's half-past eight!!"

I told her I hadn't been asleep AT ALL, ALL NIGHT, and that it was HER FAULT because she should have let me open just ONE present.

Mum said not to worry because now I could open ALL my presents . . . !

ONCE I'd opened ALL my birthday cards.

The **trouble with being made to open your birthday cards before you've opened your presents** is birthday cards aren't anywhere near as good as presents.

Mum says that cards are important because they have birthday messages in and they tell you who the presents are from.

I got a Shaker Maker painting set from my Auntie Sue and Uncle Clive.

I got a SlippySlidy water slide that

you can squirt washing-up liquid on from my nanny and grampy, except our garden doesn't slope very much, so it won't be very slidy. It should still be quite slippy though.

Mrs Pike, my neighbour, bought me a big book on cats.

And Mum bought me a new second-hand bike! With bigger wheels and a higher saddle, plus a basket on the front to put things in, PLUS a drinks bottle full of orange squash, which is my favourite allowed drink.

But my best birthday present was my surprise birthday trip to the ZOO!

With Gabby and Dylan!

I'd known for ages I was going to have a special birthday treat, but I didn't know till this morning that I was going to be going to the ZOO!

With Dylan and Gabby too!!

Mum told me when I was eating my breakfast. I was so excited, one of my cornflakes went down sideways!

And then things got even more exciting!!!

I thought Dylan and Gabby were the extra-special secret surprise bit of my birthday treat, but I was wrong!

Dylan and Gabby coming to the zoo with me was only just one little bit of the extra-special secret surprise!

The biggest bit of my extra-special secret birthday surprise was . . .

You're never going to guess . . .

Go on, guess . . .

You'll never guess . . .

Have you guessed?

I bet you haven't.

OK, I'll tell you . . .

The biggest bit of my special secret birthday zoo surprise was . . .

I was going to FEED THE PENGUINS AT THE ZOO!

My mum had actually arranged

for me to go into the actual penguin cage with the actual zoo keeper and FEED actual penguins on my birthday! REAL ACTUAL PENGUINS! With actual beaks and everything!

How brilliant is that! Gabby and Dylan were coming to our house at 10:00, and then the three of us were going to spend a whole day at the zoo together.

Plus my mum.

PLUS, out of the WHOLE ZOO, I would be the ONLY ONE out of absolutely everyone that would be allowed to feed the actual penguins in the actual penguin cage today!

How totally totally brilliant is that!

Mum said she was pleased that I was pleased about my extra-special surprise. Then she pointed at the floor and asked if I'd like to do something extra-special for her before we got ready to go out.

That's the **trouble with birthday wrapping paper**. It always needs picking up afterwards.

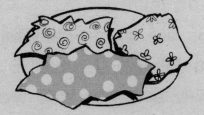

Chapter 4

The **trouble with waiting by the window for your best friends to turn up** is they never turn up when you want them to.

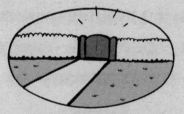

I was ready at half-past nine. Why couldn't they be too?

Mum told me to stop steaming up the glass or I'd have to clean the window with a duster.

That's the **trouble with breathing when you're excited**. Your teeth get too hot.

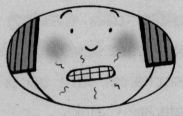

The rest of me was getting quite hot too. That's the **trouble with having your birthday in March**.

You have to put far more clothes on when you go out for birthday treats.

If my birthday was in the summer, I could have just worn flip-flops and shorts.

And a T-shirt.

And knickers.

And socks . . .

Actually, not socks.

Not with flip-flops anyway.

Anyway, anyway, Mum told me to take my duffle coat and scarf off and wait until Gabby and Dylan arrived before I put them on again, but I wouldn't, because I wanted to make sure I was extra–extra ready. Being extra-extra ready is really good.

When Dylan and Gabby arrived at my house, they had their coats and scarves on too.

Gabby was wearing her Wellingtons as well, just in case there was any elephant poo at the zoo.

The **trouble with treading in elephant poo** is it can go right up past your knees if you're not careful. Up to your head if you're really little!

So I put my Wellingtons on too, just in case, but Dylan didn't.

Dylan said he wasn't scared and was going in his shoes! He is nine though.

In the car on the way to the zoo, I opened my presents from Gabby and Dylan.

Gabby bought me a magic set, and Dylan gave me a rocket for letting off on the lawn plus a real actual snake skin. He said he found it in his snake tank and it came off his snake, who's called Shooter.

When I wiggled the snake skin at Gabby, she screamed and bashed it with her hand.

So it broke in half.

That's the **trouble with snake skins**: they're not meant to be bashed.

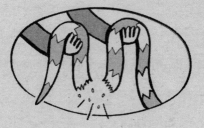

Dylan said he couldn't wait to visit the reptile house and Gabby said she was bursting to see the monkeys.

But I wanted to see the PENGUINS!

When I told Gabby and Dylan that I was actually going to feed actual penguins with actual fish out of an actual bucket, they were really jealous!

Gabby said, "Woww!" and Dylan said, "Coool!"

Then my mum said we'd have to go back to the house because she'd forgotten our tickets.

That's the **trouble with mums when they go to zoos**: they need to get more organized.

On the way back to our house, we sang Nelly the Elephant, but instead of shouting trump trump trump, we did great big elephant-poo noises! Mum let us because it was my birthday, but asked if we could sing something nicer on the way back to the zoo. No one knew any nice songs so we did animal noises instead.

The **trouble with doing animal noises** is zoo animals are really hard.

Farm animals are easy, but zoo animals aren't. No one knew what noise a rhinoceros made, or a zebra or a camel or a crocodile or even a penguin!

Gabby knew how to do monkeys and Dylan knew how to do snakes, but the only one I could think of was a lion.

Then Gabby had a brilliant idea. Why not do the sounds of a lion eating a monkey and a snake!

So we did!

Then we did the sounds of a monkey eating a snake and a lion!

But the funniest one was the sound of a snake eating a lion and a monkey!

With squirty cream!

I did the squirty-cream sound, plus the lion, and then Dylan did the sound of the snake plus some CUSTARD TOO!!

It was sooooo funny I nearly wet myself!

Mum said it was sooooo noisy too, then asked us if we would mind making the sounds of a giraffe instead.

None of us knew what a giraffe sounded like, so Mum said, "Actually, giraffes don't make any sounds at all."

Which is silly.

And impossible.

So we all made hairy gorilla noises instead.

Mum said we were getting over-excited, which wasn't true. But when we started doing dinosaur noises, she said if we didn't stop, then she would.

When we asked her what she meant, she said that if we didn't stop doing dinosaur noises right there and then, she would stop the car right there and then.

So we stopped.

And she kept going.

Chapter 5

When we got to the zoo, there were loads of people there already.

We had to drive for miles to find a parking space, but I didn't care. There might have been lots of people there already but I was the only one who was going to be allowed to feed the actual penguins!

The **trouble with actual penguins** is you can't just feed them when you want to.

Mum said I had to wait till feeding time, which wasn't until two o'clock!

I said they were bound to be hungry right now, and if I didn't get to feed them right away, they would probably starve to death.

Mum said they wouldn't starve to death at all and there were plenty of other animals to look at in the meantime.

Dylan wanted to go straight to the snakes, but I didn't mind where we went, and anyway the monkey house was nearest.

The **trouble with monkey houses** is they really pong. Gabby says it's the smell of you-know-what, but Dylan said it was mouldy bananas as well.

The **trouble with mouldy bananas** is they go all brown and squidgy.

My mum put one in my lunch box once, but I refused to eat it. She said it wasn't mouldy, and if I'd taken the trouble to peel it, I would have found a perfectly good banana inside.

But Gabby said if you try to peel a mouldy banana, it will explode all over your face and your school clothes, so there was no way I was going to eat it. Not even if someone tried to force me.

Monkeys don't care about exploding bananas. That's because they don't wear school clothes or even go to school.

The **trouble with going to school if you're a monkey** is you're not allowed to jump around in class.

Or swing from ropes or throw orange peel on the floor.

Jack Beechwhistle threw a crisp packet on the floor in the playground once and he got told off by the dinner lady. And he had to pick it up.

There's no way I would have invited Jack Beechwhistle to the zoo with me today.

Not unless we could have fed him to the lions.

The **trouble with lions** is they lie down too much.

At least zoo lions do. You can watch monkeys for ages because they never stop swinging around or climbing on tyres or scratching their bottoms. But lions don't have any ropes or tyres to play with. All they have is about two rocks.

They always look really puffed

out though. Except you can never tell why. Telly lions are always racing after zebras and stuff, which would definitely puff you out because zebras are really fast runners. But zoo lions never seem to do anything. Apart from twitch their tails. If you ask me, all zoo lions seem to do is lie down all the time and blink a lot.

And they've got flies on their face. Me and Gabby counted thirteen flies on one daddy lion's face.

Actually, I counted fifteen, but Gabby said I'd counted some of my flies twice.

The **trouble with counting flies on lions' faces** is the flies never stay still.

Only the lion does. One moment the flies are crawling around its eyes, the next minute they're crawling up its nose.

Gabby says lions' faces are covered in meat juice. The **trouble with meat juice** is if you don't wash it off, you get flies all over you.

Because meat juice is really attractive to flies. If lions washed their faces and paws after they'd had their zebra, they'd be all right. Trouble is, lions don't know how to use a flannel or pick up soap.

Dylan said that chameleons eat flies; so do tree frogs and so do little iguanas. So we went to the reptile house next.

Chapter 6

The **trouble with reptile houses** is it's really dark inside.

Gabby said it was spooky, and my mum said she couldn't see where she was going. Then Dylan said we weren't inside the reptile bit yet. We were just in the bit you have to go through first.

When we opened the next door, it got bright again, and you could see lots of different tanks made of glass. That's what reptiles live in – glass tanks instead of cages, otherwise they'll crawl through the bars and get you.

There were all sorts of different lizards in the glass tanks, and snakes and even great big frogs. They didn't do very much either, though. In fact, the snakes looked even stiller than the lions.

Gabby said it was probably because it was so hot inside. She said if she lived somewhere that was as hot as a reptile house, all she would do is lie down and eat ice creams.

Dylan said snakes don't eat ice creams and they were probably saving their energy for when they had to pounce on a locust or something else they wanted to eat. Locusts are like big grasshoppers, except they taste of Africa.

The **trouble with tasting of Africa** is that there are loads of animals that want to eat you: lions, tigers, leopards, cheetahs. But not tortoises.

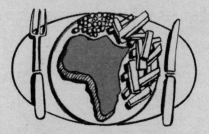

Tortoises only eat lettuce, which doesn't taste of anything. I know because I had some at my nanny and grampy's once.

The tortoises in the reptile house were being too still as well, so I tapped on their glass with my hand.

"Don't tap on the glass, Daisy," said Mum, pointing to a sign on the glass tank that said, PLEASE DO NOT TAP ON THE GLASS.

The **trouble with not tapping on the glass in the reptile house** is you'll never get anything to move.

My mum said that every time we turned round the tortoises quickly jumped up and did cartwheels behind our backs.

But each time we turned round really quickly to try and catch them out, they still looked just as still. So we went to look at some other animals.

Chapter 7

The **trouble with sparrows** is it's a swizz putting them in a zoo.

When we went to look at the spider monkeys, there were sparrows in the cage too! They were flying around and perching on branches and pecking at the floor and everything. Who wants to see sparrows in a zoo? You can see them in your own garden at home.

If you ask me, zoos should let all their sparrows go and put something better in the cages instead. Like budgies!

Gabby said they might be African sparrows. But they looked like normal ones to me.

The **trouble with spider monkeys** is their heads look too small.

Plus their tails look too long. Mum said that spider monkeys can use their tails just like people use their arms and legs. Their tails are really strong, which means they can hang upside down from branches and peel kiwi fruits at the same time.

I still can't see why they've got such small heads though . . .

Gabby said they probably fell from a tree when they were hanging by their tails. If you fall from a tree when you're hanging by your tail, your head will hit the ground and get banged down into your shoulders. That would definitely make your head look really small.

Dylan said they were just weird.

Not as weird as a fossa though. Me, Gabby and Dylan had never heard of a fossa before. Even my mum hadn't heard of a fossa, and she's heard of everything! But fossas do exist because we nearly actually saw one. And boy, do they look weird!

They've got the whiskers of an otter, the nose of a dog, the tail of a cat and the smooth brown body of an ottercatdog!! How weird is that?

The **trouble with fossas** is they hide a lot, which means that if you look through the glass, you don't actually get to see an actual fossa.

You can see the actual picture of them on the cage, though.

Mum said that fossas are like ugly tree lions, and they can chase through trees just like a squirrel. Except they don't chase nuts. They chase lemurs!

To eat!

Gabby reckons fossas eat cars, too, because there were two dead tyres on the floor of the fossa's cage. All the rest of the car had been eaten! Dylan said there was no way that any animal could eat a car. Except for a tyrannosaurus rex. But me and Gabby definitely reckoned the fossa tyres had been chewed.

Then we looked for bits of dead lemur. But we couldn't see any. So we went to look at the alive ones.

The **trouble with alive lemurs** is they look like spider monkeys.

Plus they haven't got any thumbs. Not proper thumbs like proper humans anyway. Mum said that they'd be no good at hitchhiking. But we didn't know what she meant. Then she said that considering they didn't have proper thumbs, they were really good at peeling oranges.

There were dead bits of actual fruit all over the lemurs' floor.

The **trouble with dead bits of actual fruit** is they make the cage look really untidy.

Mum said the floor of the lemur cage reminded her of the floor in my bedroom. Which is a lie, because the only fruit I've ever left on my carpet is about three apple cores.

And a banana skin.

But not a mouldy one. And not all at the same time either. Like a lemur would.

Plus I don't like kiwi fruit. It's got too many pips.

The **trouble with pips** is they don't taste very nice.

If you had lemur teeth, they'd probably taste all right, but if you've got normal teeth, then they don't taste very nice at all. Especially if you crunch one.

My mum bought a big bunch of grapes from the supermarket once and they were full of pips. In fact, there were more pips than grape! She said she'd meant to buy pipless grapes, but the supermarket was closing so she'd just grabbed the nearest ones.

The **trouble with just grabbing the nearest ones** is you can end up spitting pips out for ages.

Mum only buys pipless grapes now. But mostly she buys apples.

Or bananas. And tangerines at Christmas. But not kiwis.

Because of the pips.

Chapter 8

After the lemurs we went to see the llamas.

The **trouble with llamas** is they might spit at you even if they're not eating grapes!

My mum says llamas only spit at people when they're frightened, and the thing to do is watch their ears. If the ears of a llama go back, then it means they're going to spit and you should run away as fast as you can.

Gabby reckons llamas only spit at people who call them names. They'd probably spit at Jack Beechwhistle then, 'cos he's always calling people names.

I bet if he saw a llama, he'd call it Goofy or something, just because its teeth stick out and look all funny. Jack Beechwhistle called Melanie Beamish "Bugs Bunny" once at school, and her teeth hardly stick out at all. She didn't spit at him, though. We're not allowed to do spits at school. She whacked him on the back with her lunch box instead.

Dylan says animal teeth have different designs, depending on what sort of food they eat. Lions have biting teeth, hyenas have crunching teeth, giraffes have munching teeth and humming birds have sucking teeth. Which you can't actually see because they're so small.

Elephants have the biggest teeth. Did you know an elephant's tooth is the size of a brick and weighs three kilos! That's heavier than a flower pot! It's definitely true because it said so on the sign on the wall outside the elephant cage.

Imagine being a tooth fairy and having to pick up an elephant's tooth! Gabby reckons it would take about twenty tooth fairies all at once to pick up an elephant's tooth. I reckon tooth fairies have special fairy cranes for doing really heavy zoo jobs.

There were loads of signs on the walls at the zoo. At first I didn't take much notice of them because the animals were too exciting, but when we went to see the sea lions, the whole wall was covered in signs!

Mum said they weren't signs, they were plaques, and each plaque meant that someone had adopted a sea lion. She said that zoos liked visitors to adopt their animals because it helped the zoo to look after them.

Loads of people had adopted the sea lions. I reckon it's because they've got really cute faces.

And they're really good swimmers. Mum said that sea lions have special nostrils that close tightly when they put their whiskers under the water. Sea-lion nostrils are so good they can stay under water for forty minutes! So can the rest of the sea lion!!

I tried holding my breath under-water in the bath once, but I could only do it for about one second. Plus the water went up my nose. That's because I haven't got sea-lion nostrils. Or a snorkel.

The **trouble with snorkels** is my mum won't let me have one.

Or a deep-sea diving suit. I saw a deep-sea diver on the telly once and it was really good.

If you've got a deep-sea diving suit, you get to do lots of roly-polys backwards off of boats. And you get to swim with actual sharks.

The **trouble with actual sharks** is they'd be better if they only had sucking teeth.

If sharks had sucking teeth like a humming bird instead of biting teeth like a lion, then they wouldn't look so scary. Plus they wouldn't be able to chomp you, they'd only be able to suck you.

Whales only suck, and they don't look scary at all. Even great big whales don't look scary. They always look gentle and kind.

The **trouble with trying to fit a whale in a zoo** is there wouldn't be any space for any other animals.

Apart from leaf-cutter ants. That's why you never see whales in zoos.

Chapter 9

About the biggest thing you can fit in a zoo is an elephant. Then it's a rhinoceros.

The **trouble with rhinoceroses** is they should go to the loo before the zoo opens.

Gabby, Dylan and me were looking down over the wall into the great big space where they lived, when the rhino did the most ginormous disgusting wee! It was so ginormous and so disgusting that we had to close our eyes.

We closed our eyes and counted to ten, but when we opened them again, it was still doing it!

Dylan reckoned it did enough wee to fill two paddling pools! I reckon rhinos should be banned if they're going to do things like that in front of children on their birthday.

Mum said that when you're a rhino, you can just do what you want when you want. Because no one's going to stop you.

The **trouble with trying to stop a rhino** is they're made out of concrete.

If you try and stop a rhino doing a wee or anything, it will run you over and squash you flat or bash you up into the air with its horn.

Dylan said a rhino's horn isn't made out of concrete, it's made out of hair. Special hairy concrete-type hair that you only get in Africa.

Anyway, even if a rhino horn really is only made out of hair, it can still give you a really hard bash.

The other **trouble with white rhinos** is they're not that white.

The sign said it was a "White Rhino", but the one at our zoo was brown.

Gabby said it wasn't brown, it was mud, and it was probably white underneath the brown mud. I said it should stop getting so muddy or everyone would think it was a liar, but Dylan said it needed the mud for camouflage.

The **trouble with camouflage** is it makes things really hard to see.

Apart from the Nile monitor lizard. I saw him straight away.

Camouflage is like wearing special clothes that make you invisible. Lizards' camouflage is the colour of leaves, butterflies' camouflage is the colour of flower petals, zebras' camouflage is the colour of stripy grass and the Loch Ness monster's camouflage is the colour of Loch Ness.

That's why no one's ever seen it. Including deep-sea divers.

The worst kind of zoo camouflage is the flamingos. They're easy peasy to see, because flamingos aren't the same colour as anything. They're just pink. Bright pink, too! And they stand on one leg.

The **trouble with standing on one leg when you're pink** is it makes you look like a stick of candyfloss.

Dylan says if animals don't taste nice, sometimes they have really bright colours on them to warn other animals not to bite them.

I said that if I was going to warn an animal not to bite me, I'd make myself look like a pea, not something as yummy as candyfloss.

Then Mum said we should all try standing on one leg too. Dylan did it

for the longest, then me, then Gabby,
except Gabby said I pushed her but
I didn't. I just sort of fell on her, but I
couldn't help it.

Mum read the sign on the flamingo fence and told us that a flamingo can stand on one leg for up to four hours without putting its foot down. Or even wobbling!

Trouble is, we didn't really have long enough to see if it was true, because straight after the flamingos it was time for my birthday zoo lunch!

Chapter 10

I love birthday zoo lunches!

Last year, I had a birthday Wacky Playpark lunch, but birthday zoo lunches are even better!

After we had found a bench to sit on that was sort of out of the wind, Mum took our birthday zoo sandwiches out of her bag. Most of the time in my sandwiches I only get to have cheese or jam. But when it's my birthday, my mum lets me have whatever I want!

"WITHIN REASON."

Because birthday sandwiches are really special!

Dylan said he had Bully Bear in his sandwiches at school but he'd never had it with hundreds and thousands on.

Gabby said Bully Bear with hundreds and thousands on tasted really nice and she was going to try hundreds and thousands with cheese spread when she got home.

The **trouble with trying hundreds and thousands with cheese spread** is you'd better ask your mum first.

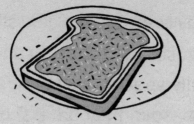

Because it needs to be your birthday really. Otherwise your mum will probably say, "No, you can't have hundreds and thousands on your cheese spread. Are you mad? Put the hundreds and thousands back in the cupboard right now."

I was nearly going to have special birthday mini sausages dipped in chocolate spread too. But I tried them at home, and they weren't very nice. So I didn't.

Gabby said she was glad she didn't have to try sausages in chocolate spread, and that sometimes things are nicer when they are just ordinary.

That's why we had ordinary sausages and cheesy puffs not dipped in anything. And we had chicken saté sticks AND we had lemonade (which is my favourite not-allowed drink)!

While we were sitting on the bench eating our lunch, loads of birds started coming all around us. There were sparrows that had escaped out of their cages, plus about seven pigeons, three ducks and a yellow tit. Except Mum said it was a greenfinch.

Except it didn't look very green to me.

Dylan said that in the winter, birds find it really hard to find food. That's why people hang peanuts up in their gardens.

Gabby said the birds had definitely smelled our Bully Bear with hundreds and thousands on, and we had better eat our sandwiches fast!

The **trouble with eating your sandwiches fast** is if you're not careful, you might choke.

I was really careful because I didn't want to drop any of my hundreds and thousands, but Gabby wasn't careful at all.

So she ended up choking all over the place. And scaring the birds.

AND she had to borrow some of my lemonade to wash her sandwich down. Which wasn't fair because she'd already had her own lemonade. Plus I like lemonade more than she does.

And it was my birthday, not hers.

Which means I should have got the most lemonade out of everyone.

But I didn't.

Because of Gabby's chokes.

Which isn't fair. But it ended up all right. Because Mum said I could have some more lemonade when we got home.

After Gabby had stopped choking, we had chocolate mini rolls.

The **trouble with chocolate mini rolls** is they're not as big as a proper birthday cake.

They do taste really nice, though! Mum said Nanny and Grampy were coming to see me when we got back from the zoo and Nanny was going to bring a special zoo birthday cake that she had baked all by herself, with an apron and everything!

Gabby said it was probably a good idea to have my big cake later, because if elephants sniffed a big cake, it would make them stampede all over us.

Stampedes are when loads of animals break out of their cages and run at you to get your cake.

Dylan said he saw a stampede of cows in a film once and they ran over everything, including bushes, fences and a river. Plus they flattened a cowboy.

He was probably the one holding the cake.

I wonder if it was his birthday too?

Chapter 11

The **trouble with putting birthday candles on a chocolate mini roll** is it's really hard to fit seven candles on.

Even five is hard. Plus when you stick the candles in, the chocolate on the outside starts to break off.

Mum said I might have to settle for one candle instead of seven, but I said I wanted seven candles –

otherwise people might think I was one, which is a baby.

The **trouble with trying to light seven candles on a mini roll after you've managed to fit them on** is the wind keeps blowing them out before you get a chance to blow.

Or even huff.

Or sing "Happy Birthday".

Which is really a nuisance.

Plus the candles go wonky.

Then the chocolate starts to melt.

Then the mini roll goes sticky.

Which is all right if you're the one who's holding it, because then you get to lick the chocolate off your fingers. But if your mum is holding it, then she gets to lick her fingers instead.

Which isn't fair, because it's not her mini roll in the first place. It's mine. So I should be the one that gets to lick the chocolate off.

Mum said if I didn't stop moaning about melted chocolate, she would feed all our mini rolls to the monkeys!

Which was a lie. Because if she

did, there would be a stampede. Which would be her fault, not mine.

Then she'd get into trouble, not me.

And anyway, the wind suddenly stopped blowing.

"QUICK, QUICK, QUICK!" said Mum. "BLOW, BLOW, BLOW!"

So I did!

After I'd blown out my candles, Mum, Gabby and Dylan sang "Happy Birthday", and then Mum gave them each a mini roll too.

But not with candles. Because it wasn't their birthday.

Plus theirs weren't sticky.

When I asked my mum if I could have one that wasn't sticky as well, she said one mini roll was enough, and if I ate too many mini rolls, the zoo keeper would think I was an elephant.

Which isn't true either. Because I haven't got a trunk.

Or massive teeth.

Anyway, there weren't any more mini rolls left.

So we had apples.

The **trouble with apples** is I had one with a maggot in once.

It came off a tree in my nanny and grampy's garden. Luckily I didn't bite through the maggot, I only bit through its hole. But it still wasn't very nice.

I do still like apples because they're juicy, but I always double-check for maggot holes before I eat one now.

Especially if I'm at my nanny and grampy's house.

When we'd finished our apples, Mum looked at her watch and then put all our rubbish into a bag.

"I think we should make our way over in the direction of the penguins, don't you, Daisy?" smiled Mum.

"Yes, yes, yes, yes, yes!" said me!

Chapter 12

The **trouble with zoo bins** is sometimes they get really full. We had to really squeeze our apple cores in to stop them falling back out onto the ground.

But then Gabby's fell out again.

And then Dylan's fell out when Gabby put hers back in.

So in the end Mum put all our

apple cores back in the bag, and said she would take our rubbish home.

After we'd visited the litter bin, we went to look at the meerkats.

The **trouble with meerkats** is, WATCH OUT IF YOU'RE A SCORPION OR A SNAKE!

Because if a meerkat catches you, it will gobble you up!

Lots of people had adopted the meerkats. That's because meerkats are really good.

It said on the sign next to the adopting plaques that meerkats are immune to deadly poison! That means that even if a snake bites and bites and bites them or a scorpion stings and stings and stings them, the meerkat will just eat the snake or scorpion anyway. Without being poisoned or even getting a tummy-ache!

Dylan said he wouldn't let a meerkat anywhere near the snake tank in his bedroom.

And Gabby wondered whether meerkats could eat swede without dying too.

The next sign we saw was for the pygmy goats. The **trouble with pygmy goats** is their poos look like currants, which could be really dangerous if you were making cakes in the zoo.

Dylan said he didn't think zoos made cakes, in case of the stampedes, so we were probably safe, but Gabby said that in future if she ever went into a zoo shop to buy something to eat, she would never buy a currant cake in case it had a pygmy-goat poo in it. In fact, just to be totally safe she was going to totally stick to ice creams.

The **trouble with ice creams** is it's really hard to get your mum to buy you one when it's March.

Especially if you've already had mini rolls and lemonade. Mum said it was too cold for ice creams, and anyway we'd all had a birthday zoo lunch.

The **trouble with birthday zoo lunches** is they really make you need an ice cream. Especially MY birthday zoo lunches.

It took me about ten minutes to persuade Mum that we all really really really needed ice creams. At first she wouldn't listen, but in the end she did a big sigh and she said we just had time to go to buy some, before we went to the penguins.

The **trouble with ice-cream cabinets in zoo shops on March 3rd** is there aren't any ice creams in them.

There isn't anything in them at all! Apart from cold air.

The lady behind the counter said ice creams were out of season and they wouldn't be getting any in until Easter.

So we had to have sweets instead.

The **trouble with sweets** is you're not allowed to feed them to the animals.

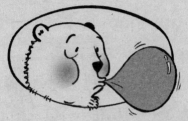

I saw some white-nosed coatis who really looked like they wanted a Tic-Tac, but Mum said all the animals in the zoo were on carefully controlled diets that didn't include Tic-Tacs, Refreshers or Hubba Bubba bubble gum.

I said if they liked fruit, they were bound to like strawberry

Hubba Bubba, but Mum gave me one of her looks and said if we couldn't control our sweets, then we would have to put them in her handbag for safekeeping.

Then she looked at her watch.

IT WAS TIME TO FEED THE PENGUINS!

Chapter 13

My heart was beating really fast when we arrived at the penguin house. Mum said hers was too, but that was because she isn't used to running.

When we got there, a zoo man in a brown uniform with a zoo badge on it was waiting for us by the gate.

"Are you Daisy?" he asked.

"Yes!" said my mum, pointing to me. "Sorry we're late!"

"That's fine," said the zoo man. "My name's Tim. Happy birthday, Daisy! Would you like to feed the penguins?"

"YES, PLEASE!" I said.

"Then come with me," said Tim, "and I'll introduce you to Tiffany."

I thought Tiffany was going to be the penguin leader. But she wasn't. She was a zoo lady. Tiffany had a brown uniform with a zoo badge too, plus she was wearing Wellingtons. That's because everyone who's an expert on penguins wears Wellingtons.

Mum asked me if I wanted her to come with me, but I said no because she wasn't wearing Wellingtons.

The **trouble with not wearing Wellingtons** is penguins won't really like you.

So I told Mum it would probably be better if she went to sit with Gabby and Dylan. You can still watch penguins being fed if you haven't got Wellingtons, and they will still like you a bit. But not as much, because they're only liking you through the glass.

Mum took Gabby and Dylan into the bit behind the glass where they could sit and watch me and the penguins, and then Tiffany held my hand.

Then my heart started beating EVEN FASTER because I was actually going in!

Right in!! Into the penguin house. With the actual penguins!!!!!!!

First of all we went down a slope, then up a bit to a gate that had two padlocks and two bolts on it. Tiffany undid the padlocks and then opened the gate. I couldn't see any penguins at first because

Tiffany's zoo shirt was in the way.
But when we walked right inside
through the gate, there were
penguins all over the place!

Plus there was a baby penguin
too!

Chapter 14

The **trouble with baby penguins** is they can't really do very much. Except sort of stand still.

Tiffany said that baby penguins don't get their proper feathers until they are about six months old, which means they can't swim around like their mummies and daddies can.

Mummy and daddy penguins have

special swimming feathers that keep water out and stop them getting soggy. Baby penguins don't have proper feathers at all. All baby penguins have is fluff.

Which doesn't keep water out.

But it does make them look reeeeaaaaallly cute.

Tiffany knew loads about penguins. When she was opening the penguin cupboard, she said there were eighteen different types of penguin in the world. Not including the chocolate biscuit ones.

The ones we were going to feed were called Humboldt penguins.

Which isn't a very good name for a
type of penguin, I think.

Plus it's really hard to spell.

Anyway, when the mummy and
daddy penguins saw Tiffany open

the cupboard, they started jumping off the rocks and diving into the pool. Then they started zooming through the water and doing sort of sideways roly-polys.

Tiffany said they looked really hungry, and then she asked me if I was any good at throwing fish.

I said I was really good, which was a bit of a fib because I'd never thrown a fish before. I'd thrown tennis balls and frisbees in the park, and I threw a stone at school once, but I got told off for doing that.

Anyway, I just knew I'd be really good at throwing fish.

Then I saw Mum through the glass on the other side of the pool! And Gabby and Dylan! They were sitting in the middle of a huge crowd of people and they were waving.

I waved back, and then my mum got her camera out to take a picture.

The **trouble with saying "cheese" when you're about to feed the penguins** is you can't really.

Otherwise the penguins might think you're going to feed them cheese and not fish. Penguins don't like cheese. It's not fishy enough.

The only thing that's fishy enough for penguins is actual fish.

The **trouble with saying "fish" when you're having your photo taken** is it makes your lips look funny. Which spoils the picture.

So I didn't say anything. I just smiled at my mum's camera instead. And waved.

Then Tiffany brought me a bucket! Not a red plastic bucket like our one at home, but a proper zoo bucket made especially for penguins out of real metal.

"Here you go, Daisy!" said Tiffany. "Make sure they all get their fair share!"

Then I looked inside the bucket.

Well, you should have seen how many fish there were inside! There were dead fish right up to the top!

Chapter 15

At first I thought they were alive fish in the bucket, but they weren't. They were all dead and silver with red eyes. That's just how penguins like them.

When I picked the first fish up, it felt a bit cold and slippery. I only picked it up by its tail. Just in case it WAS still alive. Plus I didn't know what it would feel like.

The **trouble with dead fish** is they feel a bit strange at first. Even if you only pick them up by the tail.

The **trouble with picking a dead fish up by the tail** is it makes it quite hard to throw.

My first fish didn't go anywhere near where I meant it to, but a penguin still got it anyway. In fact, THREE penguins zoomed right after it but only one managed to get it.

Everyone in the crowd cheered when the fish got gobbled! So next time I threw two fish at once!!

You should have seen the penguins then! I never knew they could swim so fast. The fish were only in the water for about a second before both of them had been gobbled up!!

Then I threw three fish at once, and they got gobbled up really quickly too!!!

After about five throws I was putting my fingers right into the bucket, right round the dead fish and everything. Without them feeling cold or slippery at all!

I'd really got the
hang of throwing,
and I was making
the penguins zoom
absolutely every-
where!

The penguins must have been
REALLY hungry because the more
I threw, the more they dived and
zoomed.

 One penguin
even got out
of the pool to
try and steal a
fish OUT OF MY
BUCKET!

Everyone laughed, and Tiffany had to shoo him straight back into the pool.

It was soooooooo brilliant! Everyone was cheering and clapping, and there were bubbles coming out of the water, and splashes, and really fast beaks zooming everywhere.

Plus I was a really good thrower. Just like I said I would be.

When I did my second-best throw, it went right across into the corner of the penguin pool. But my BEST throw was SOOOO good, it went right over the pool, through the air and hit the glass on the other side, where Mum,

Gabby and Dylan were sitting. Everyone really laughed and clapped then!

Gabby and Dylan thought it was hilarious!

My mum tried to take a picture. But she missed it.

That's the **trouble with mums taking good pictures**. They're a bit slow.

So then I tried to throw a fish right out of the zoo! But I only had three fish left in my bucket, and they were really slippery ones. Plus one didn't have a head. So they only went as far as the middle.

But Mum still took a picture. And everyone still clapped! And the penguins kept diving and zooming around.

Then my bucket ran out.

The **trouble with buckets running out** is you don't have any fish left to throw.

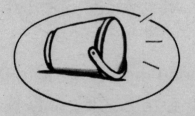

Which isn't very good, because the penguins still looked really hungry.

So I threw the bucket into the penguin pool too.

I didn't actually mean to throw the bucket in – it just sort of came out of my hands. I wasn't trying to throw it in on purpose or anything. I just thought there might be some fish juice left in the bottom and the penguins might like to lick it out.

Penguins love fish juice.

The **trouble with zoo buckets** is that they sink. Because they're metal.

Plus if they land on a penguin, they can give it a really big bump on the head.

Luckily all the penguins dived out of the way, but the zoo bucket sank right to the bottom of the water.

At first everyone laughed and cheered. Except my mum. Mum covered her eyes and went red, but most people thought it was funny. Gabby and Dylan thought it was hilaaaaaaaaaaaaaaaaaaaarious!

I'm not sure if Tiffany did, though. She sort of smiled and sort of frowned at the same time. And then she had to go and get a long zoo net.

The **trouble with zoo nets** is they're not very good at picking up buckets.

Which meant Tiffany had to spend quite a long time trying to get the bucket out. I asked her if she wanted me to have a go, but she said it would be better if I left it to her.

So I did.

It would definitely have been better if she had let me have a go with the net, because I'm really expert at that too.

In Cornwall when I was on holiday, Mum bought me a net. When I put it in the rock pool, I caught loads of sand, two shells and a lolly stick on my very first go! I nearly caught some weed too, but it escaped when I lifted the net up.

Tiffany took loads of goes before she even caught anything.

By the time she'd put the bucket back in the penguin cupboard and taken me back to Mum, Dylan and Gabby, most of the people behind the glass had gone. Mum said the elephants were being fed at 2:30 and everyone had probably gone to see them.

Plus she said sorry to Tiffany.

Tiffany said it was OK and she hoped I'd had a good time.

I said I'd had a REALLY good time.

Tiffany said I was SO good at throwing fish I'd be after her job one day. Then she asked me if I would like her job one day?

I said yes, but actually I fibbed, because I wouldn't want to do a job with a brown shirt. I wouldn't mind the badge though.

Except I think I'd want a growling lion on my badge. Not a paw print.

Then we waved goodbye to the penguins.

Chapter 16

On the way back from the penguin house, Gabby couldn't stop giggling. Dylan thought it was really funny too.

"What if you'd hit a penguin on the head?" laughed Dylan.

"What if a penguin had thought the bucket was a fish? And swallowed it!" laughed Gabby.

That's the **trouble with Gabby**.

She might have had Wellingtons on, but she's not the slightest bit expert about penguins.

Then Mum asked us where we'd like to go next.

So I said, "Home."

"HOME?" said Mum. "Surely you don't want to go home yet! We haven't seen the crocodiles, or the tigers or the vultures or the mongooses."

So I told her I was really tired.

"You're not worried about the bucket are you, Daisy?" she said. "You really shouldn't be worried about the bucket."

So I told her that the **trouble with doing really good throws** is it can really make your arms ache, and that I REALLY wanted to go home.

"REALLY?" she said.

"REALLY, REALLY," I said.

"But we haven't even seen the giraffes yet!" said Mum. "We must go and see the giraffes!"

"Yes, we have seen the giraffes," I said. "They were over on the other side of the rhinoceros bit."

"Well, we haven't seen the giraffes close up," said Mum.

My mum really likes giraffes.

I said we didn't need to see a giraffe close up, because they're so tall. You can see a giraffe from anywhere.

So Mum sighed, and then asked Gabby and Dylan what they wanted to do.

Gabby said she wanted to go to the play area and Dylan said, "Are there any rhinoceros beetles?"

Which was a real nuisance, because I really wanted to go home.

Mum said if there were any

rhinoceros beetles, they were probably in the reptile house. But Dylan said rhinoceros beetles weren't reptiles, they were insects. Dylan said rhinoceros beetles are the strongest animals in the world and they can lift things that are 850 times heavier than themselves. Which IS quite cool, but I REALLY REALLY wanted to go home.

Luckily the zoo didn't have any rhinoceros beetles. They did have hissing cockroaches, but Dylan said they wouldn't be as good.

The **trouble with play areas** is the zoo DID have one of them.

When we got there, it had slides and rope bridges and tunnels and everything. Gabby and Dylan couldn't wait to go on them, but I REALLY REALLY wanted to go home.

So I sat on a bench with my mum.

"Are you sure you're feeling all right, Daisy?" asked Mum. "You love swings and slides usually. I can never get you OFF the swings and slides when we go to the park!"

I said I was feeling fine, but I REALLY REALLY REALLY wanted to go home.

Luckily there was a puddle at the bottom of the big slide.

The **trouble with big slides** is they make you come down so fast, you can't stop yourself at the bottom.

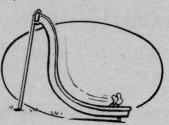

So if there's a puddle at the bottom, your bottom goes straight in it.

Gabby came down first.

And then Dylan.

You should have seen Gabby's
face. She had dirty puddle water
all over her coat and all down her
tights.

Dylan didn't get so much on him, because Gabby's bottom had already soaked a lot of the puddle up, but he still made his jeans really dirty.

Mum brushed Dylan and Gabby's bottoms down with her glove and then said that actually, it probably WAS time to go home.

Which made me really pleased.

"Have you had a good time?!" asked Mum. "Apart from the muddy bottoms!"

"YEEEESSSSSS!!!" we shouted.

"Have you had a lovely birthday, Daisy?" she asked.

"You bet!" I said.

"Come on, then," said Mum. "Let's
make our way back to the car."

Chapter 17

The **trouble with making your way back to a car** is you can never remember where you parked it.

Mum said she was sure our car was somewhere over somewhere, but when we got somewhere over somewhere, it wasn't there at all. There were so many lines of cars everywhere, we couldn't see our car anywhere.

First we walked down one row, then we walked down another row, then we thought we'd found our car, but it was someone else's, then we walked down about a hundred more rows, then we ended up back where we started, then we didn't know where we were.

In the end we did find our car, but it wasn't somewhere over somewhere, it was somewhere over somewhere totally else.

Mum said that next time she parked a car at the zoo, she was going to ask a giraffe to stand beside it.

And just to make extra sure, she was going to ask the giraffe to wave a big flag.

On the way home Dylan and Gabby wanted to do animal noises again. Gabby said she'd found out what sound a sea lion made, and Dylan said he'd learned how to do a macaw.

But I said I didn't want to play. I said I just wanted to go home.

Gabby said, "Let's sing Nelly the Elephant again", but I said I didn't want to do that either.

Mum said I must be coming down with something, and she'd "dose me up" when we got home.

I said I didn't want any medicine and I just really really needed to get home.

We were NEARLY almost totally home too, when it happened.

Chapter 18

"Mu-uuuum," I said, just as we'd turned off the roundabout near our house. "Do you think we could stop off at the shops?"

"What for, Daisy?" said Mum. "You've already had lemonade and sweets today."

So I said, "I need to buy a bag of frozen peas."

Now the **trouble with saying "I need to buy a bag of frozen peas" when your mum knows you really really don't like peas** is that your mum will get very suspicious.

"What on earth do you want with a bag of frozen peas!!?" asked Mum.

"I need it to keep my baby penguin cold," said me.

The **trouble with mums putting their foot down on a car brake really hard** is it makes everyone shoot forward really fast and it makes you think you're going to crash.

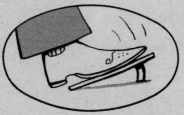

Luckily we all had our seatbelts on, but it was still really really scary and our tyres did the really realliest loudest screech ever.

"I've called him Findus," I said.

The **trouble with having a baby penguin under your duffel coat** is, well, lots of things really.

"WHAT ARE YOU DOING WITH A PENGUIN UNDER YOUR DUFFEL COAT!" screamed Mum, staring down at my lap with her mouth really really wide open.

"I've adopted him," I said.

"ADOPTED HIM!" squealed Mum. "YOU CAN'T ADOPT AN ANIMAL FROM THE ZOO!"

"Everyone else has," I said.

Then Gabby and Dylan undid their seatbelts really quickly and dived over my shoulders to have a look.

"WOW!" said Gabby.

"COOL!" said Dylan.

"Oh my God, we're going to prison," said my mum. "We've kidnapped a penguin and WE'RE GOING TO PRISON!"

"Can I stroke him?" said Gabby.

"Can I stroke him next?" said Dylan.

"When did you kidnap a penguin?"

said Mum. "HOW did you kidnap a penguin?"

"When Tiffany was getting the bucket out with the net," I said. "All the mummy and daddy penguins were zooming after the net and they'd left the baby one all alone. Tiffany wasn't looking after him, and the mummy and daddy penguins weren't looking after him, so I decided I would. And anyway, I haven't kidnapped him, I've adopted him."

"DAISY, DAISY, DAISY!" said Mum. "When people adopt animals at the zoo, they don't take them home with them! They just give the zoo some money to help look after them. Looking after animals is a very expensive business and adopting an animal is just a kind and helpful way of making sure all the zoo animals are well cared for.

"NO ONE TAKES ADOPTED ANIMALS HOME!"

"Christopher Dowsett is adopted," I said. "And he lives at home."

"Christopher Dowsett isn't a zoo animal, Daisy," said Mum. "He's one of your friends at school!"

"He's still adopted," I said.

"Yes, Daisy," said Mum. "Christopher

is still adopted, but when zoos say 'adopt an animal', they don't mean adopt an animal like they mean adopt a Christopher Dowsett! They mean a different kind of adopted."

"Then they shouldn't say 'adopt an animal'," I said.

"They should say 'pay for an animal' instead.

"Or 'buy food for an animal'."

"And straw," said Gabby.

"And heat pads," said Dylan.

"Well, whatever they should say, we're taking him STRAIGHT BACK!" said Mum.

The **trouble with penguin beaks** is they can't speak.

If Findus could have talked, he would definitely have told Mum that he really really didn't want to go back to the zoo and he much preferred being with me.

"But he's all fluffy, and he's all snuggled up and his wings are all flat and nice to stroke, which means he really likes me!" I said.

"Can I have a feel?" said Gabby.

"Can I have a stroke?" said Dylan.

"I don't care how fluffy and nice he is," growled Mum. "He's going back to the zoo!"

I tried everything to stop her.

I promised I'd look after him.

I promised I'd put him in my front basket and take him for rides on my new bike.

I promised I'd get a job to pay for his fish.

I promised I'd let him sleep with me. And have baths with me, in water that wasn't too hot.

I even promised I'd take him to school with me so that he could learn how to read and write and skip and everything.

I bet none of the penguins at the zoo know how to read and write. Or skip.

But Mum still made me take Findus back.

That's **the trouble with mums whose children have adopted baby penguins**: they're just not fair!

Chapter 19

When we got back to the zoo, the zoo was on amber alert. If a lion or a rhinoceros had been missing, then it would have been a red alert, but as it was only a baby penguin, it was just an amber one.

My mum's face was on red alert though when she gave Findus back. She said it was ever so embarrassing, and she was ever so EVER SO sorry, and I hadn't meant any harm, and I'd just misunderstood what 'adopt an animal' meant.

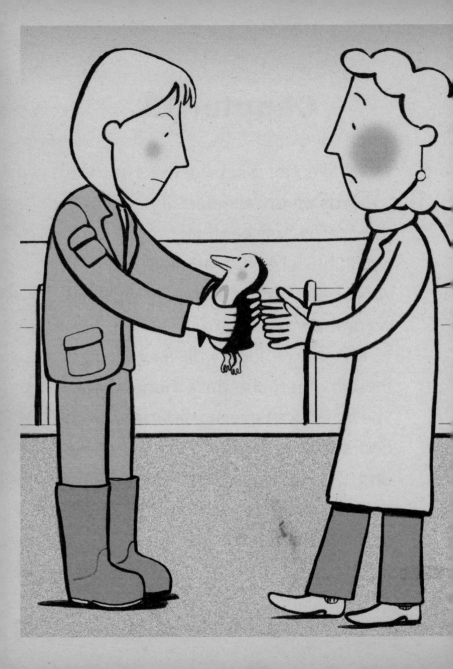

WHICH ISN'T MY FAULT!

The zoo were OK about it. They said they were just pleased to have Findus back. In fact, I'm not really sure what all the fuss was about.

After we'd dropped Gabby and Dylan off, Mum's face went all kind of strange and funny looking.

Then she started talking to herself.

"Out of all the mums in all the world, guess WHOSE daughter kidnaps a penguin from the zoo?" she said.

I decided I wouldn't say anything for a while; at least until we'd got back into the house and she'd had a cup of tea.

Trouble is, her face still looked kind of strange and funny, even after a cup of tea.

And after three crunchy creams!

So I decided I'd go upstairs to my bedroom and play with my birthday presents for a while.

The **trouble with birthday presents** is they're not as good as baby penguins.

Even magic sets with actual wands aren't as good as baby penguins.

So I wasn't really in the right mood to play with my birthday presents.

After about an hour, I went back

downstairs to see if Mum's face had got any better.

It hadn't. It had got worse.

"DAISY!" she growled. "DON'T YOU EVER STEAL A BABY PENGUIN FROM THE ZOO AGAIN!" she said. "IT'S A GOOD JOB IT'S YOUR BIRTHDAY," she said, "OR . . . OR . . . WELL, I DON'T KNOW WHAT I'D HAVE DONE."

Then her face went even stranger and funnier. Plus growlier.

"PROMISE ME, DAISY!" she said. "PROMISE ME YOU WILL NEVER STEAL A BABY PENGUIN FROM A ZOO AGAIN . . . OR A BABY CROCODILE OR A BABY ELEPHANT OR A BABY ANYTHING!"

So I promised.

I was going to double promise, but before I could say the words, our front doorbell rang.

Nanny and Grampy had arrived, with my special home-made birthday zoo cake!

Chapter 20

The **trouble with special home-made birthday zoo cakes** is sometimes the penguins on the icing look like zebras.

Especially if the person who's done them is really old. Nanny said she'd done all the penguins on the icing without copying, but apart from them being black and white, they still looked like zebras to me.

The candles looked like candles though, and I had a really good time blowing out seven more all over again!

Then everyone sang "Happy Birthday" AGAIN!

And then Nanny and Grampy gave me ANOTHER present!

Nanny said it was only something small for my new bike, but it was BRILLIANT! A real hooter that makes real loud hooting noises when you squeeze it!

Mum said it would be like living with a sea lion.

Grampy said he would fix it to my handlebars before they went home, and then he asked me to tell him all about the penguins I had fed at the zoo today.

When I looked at Mum, her face had gone a bit funny again, but then she put her finger to her lips and smiled.

So I told Nanny and Grampy about all the penguins I'd met.
(Except one.
One little one.)

Then I told them about the rhinoceros,

the lions,

the meerkats,

the flamingos,

the pygmy goats

and all the other
animals I could
remember,

including the
fossa!

And guess what? Nanny and Grampy hadn't heard of a fossa either!

They hadn't heard of loads of the things that I learned at the zoo today!

Before they left, Nanny and Grampy gave me seven birthday kisses goodbye, EACH!!

Then Mum let me have seven extra hoots on my hooter and asked me to have my bath and get ready for bed.

Before she tucked me up, she read me a story (I wanted seven, but she said no), then she stroked

my forehead and asked me to promise her again that I would NEVER adopt a zoo animal again without asking her first.

So this time I double promised.

In fact I triple promised.

But that's the **trouble with double and triple promising after you've adopted a baby penguin**.

Even if I had A ZILLION PROMISED, I still knew that Findus would be cross to be back at the penguin pool with

Tiffany and all the other penguins.

I bet you all the herrings and kippers and mackerels and sardines and pilchards and goldfish in the sea that he'd much rather have come to my house.

To live on a packet of frozen peas with me!

DAISY'S TROUBLE INDEX

The trouble with . . .

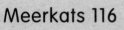

WHAT WILL DAISY DO NEXT?!